Dvarsh Workbook

Beginning Exercises
for the Extraordinary Student

by Robert Stikmanz

STIKMANTICA

AUSTIN, TEXAS

Dvarsh Workbook, Beginning Exercises for the Extraordinary Student
© 2018 by Robert D. Lewis
Cover art, book design & entire contents by Robert Stikmanz

ISBN 978-0-9838137-7-4

Cataloging Data -

Dvarsh Workbook, Beginning Exercises for the Extraordinary Student / Robert Stikmanz

       p. 60   cm.

       ISBN 978-0-9838137-7-4

       I. Stikmanz, Robert

              1. Language study—workbooks

              2. Imaginary languages in literature

              3. Invented languages—Dvarsh

              4. Fictive art

       II. Title

Stikmantica
Austin, Texas
stikmantica.com

Author's Note

Dvarsh Workbook began as a set of familiarization drills for personal use. The underlying method does not stretch beyond copying and repetition, but from simplicity and persistence will come advance.

This title is a companion to *Dvarsh, An Introduction*, abetting access to the language by presenting and demonstrating core information in bite-sized chunks. Alternatively, the exercises can serve as a set of standalone lessons for casual use. As I arranged material, the convenience of travelers to *habdvarsha* was never out of mind.

The fact that you read this note marks you apart from the crowd. Few choose paths into imaginary exile realms. You are, by an act of participation, extraordinary. Welcome to another world, a puzzle of countless solutions, and a field of play.

Robert Stikmanz

Contents

iv

Pronunciation Quick Guide

Pronunciation changes with context, and every rule has exceptions. Each consonant is itself a word, pronounced by name.

Stress. Words of two or more syllables usually stress the next to last syllable. A few stress the last syllable, indicated in writing by a doubled final consonant.

Consonants

∩	*yĕts*	**y** as in yellow
∩	*nĕth*	**n,** but **-nth** at the end of a verb infinitive.
∩	*fvē*	**fv**
∩	*psuta*	**p,** but sometimes **-ps.** Always **psuta** when a verb auxiliary.
ↄ	*habv*	**h**
ↄ	*(h)rash*	**(h)r-** or **-r,** but **-rsh** at the end of a verb infinitive.
ↄ	*mo*	**m**
ↄ	*bvĕta*	**bv,** but sometimes **b-** before ∩ [*fvē*] or ₂ [*dv'n*].
ↄ	*ch'ch*	**ch** as in church. Its verb form is the same.
ↄ	*sos*	**s** as in sun.
ↄ	*gabva*	**g** as in game.
ↄ	*aath*	**th** as in thought. Its verb form is the same.
ↄ	*lo*	**l**
ↄ	*tut*	**t**
ↄ	*wosh*	**w,** but **-wsh** at the end of a verb infinitive.
ↄ	*dza*	**dz,** but **d** when followed by ↄ [*habv*] or ∴ [ĕ].
ↄ	*jaka*	**j** as in jar.
ↄ	*ts'na*	**ts**
ↄ	*z'zl*	**z,** but **-zl** at the ends of words and some syllables.
ↄↄ	*ktho*	**kth** when followed by a vowel, but otherwise **k.**
ↄ	*shosh*	**sh** as in shush. Its verb form is the same.
ↄ	*dv'n*	**dv,** but sometimes **d.**

Vowels. Every written vowel is sounded. They are:

ₒ	**o** as in go.		∴	**ĕ** as in get.
.	**a** as in father.		,	**i** as in wit, but clipped short.
:	**ē** as in be.		ᵣ	**u** as in push.

6

Writing Dvarsh

falling				
		Yĕts		
		Nĕth		
		Fvĕ		
		Psuta		
		Habv		
		(h)Rash		
		Mo		
		Bvĕta		
		Ch'ch		
		Sos		
		Gabva		
		Aath		

rising				
		Lo		
		Tut		
		Wosh		
		Dza		
		Jaka		
		Ts'na		
		Z'zl		
		Ktho		
		Shosh		
		Dv'n		

vowels

o	ĕ
a	'
ē	u

A comparison of calligraphic and typographic characters. Reproduced from *Dvarsh, An Introduction*.

Falling characters

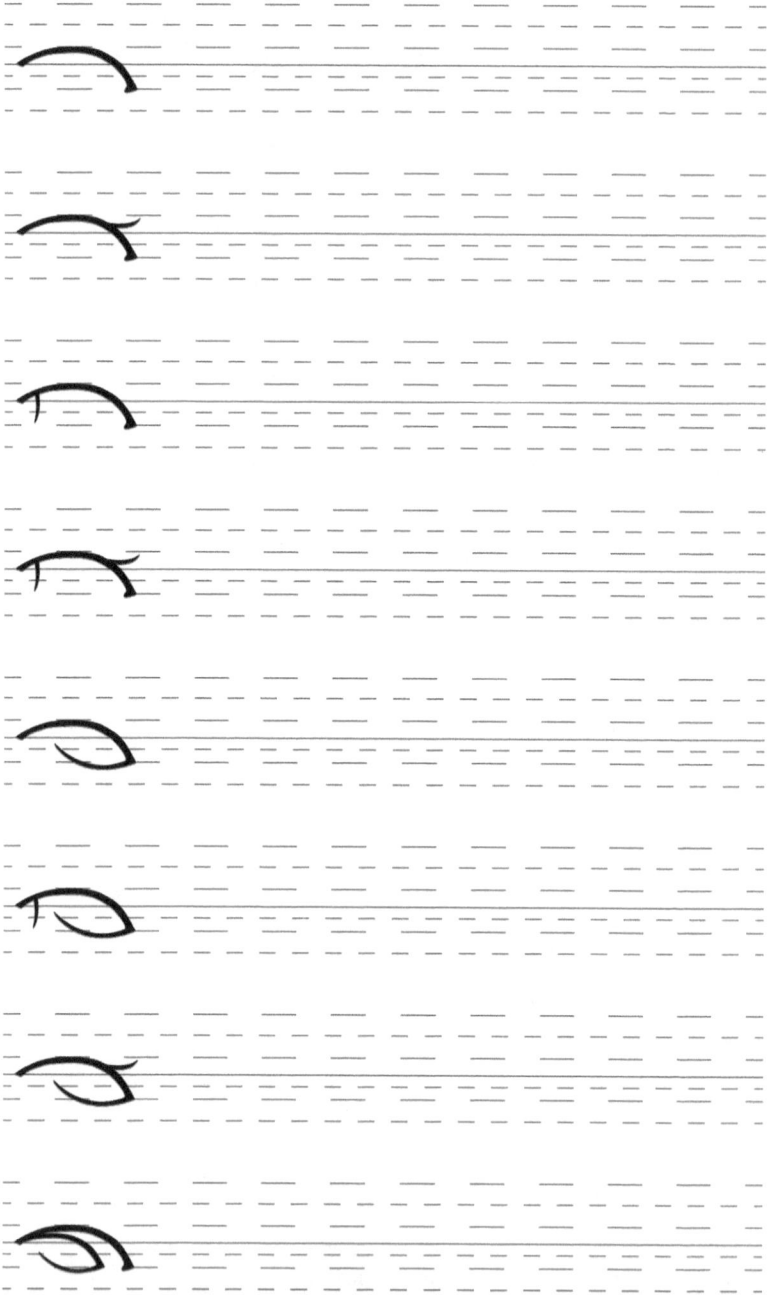

Rising characters

Vowels

Punctuation

Note: A relatively late introduction to Dvarsh, punctuation has not been embraced uniformly. Shown here are symbols most common in casual use. They are the period or full stop ["], exclamation marks [ᵇ ᵃ], the long stroke [∼ or ∾] (which can go either way), and question marks [ᶜ ᵓ]. Exclamation marks and question marks are used in pairs bracketing the affected term—i.e. *dzut!* [ᵇ ᴐᵗ↩ ᵃ]. Dvarsh convention generally places a space on both sides of any punctuation mark. The most old-fashioned scribblers may use long strokes exclusively.

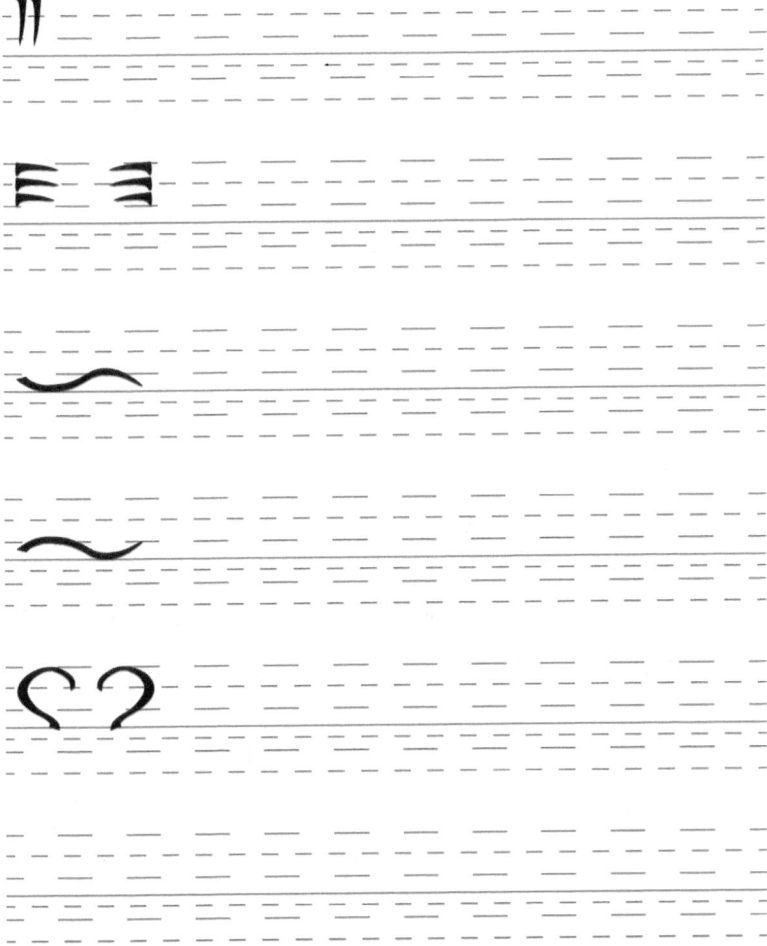

13

Numerals

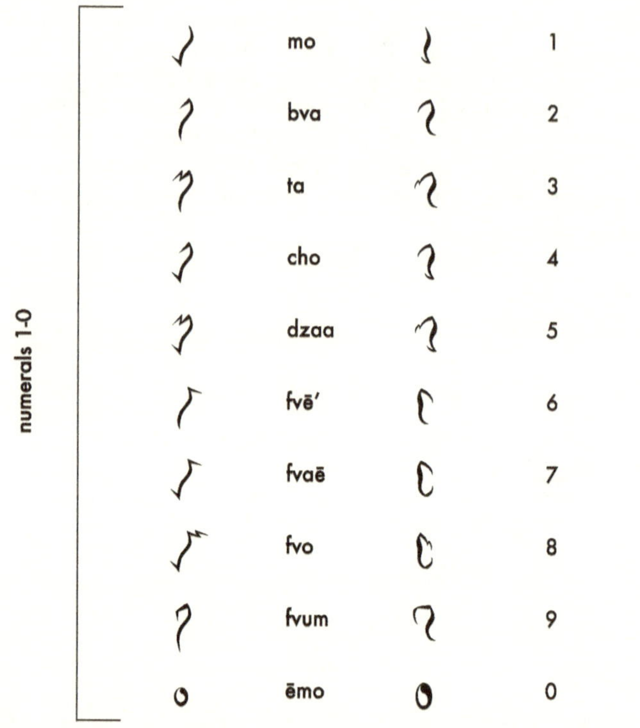
numerals 1-0
mo
1
bva
2
ta
3
cho
4
dzaa
5
fvē'
6
fvaē
7
fvo
8
fvum
9
ēmo
0

A comparison of calligraphic and typographic numerals.

The Dvarsh number system is base 10, a scheme familiar to many humans.

Written names of numbers are extremely rare. Numerals are almost always used instead.

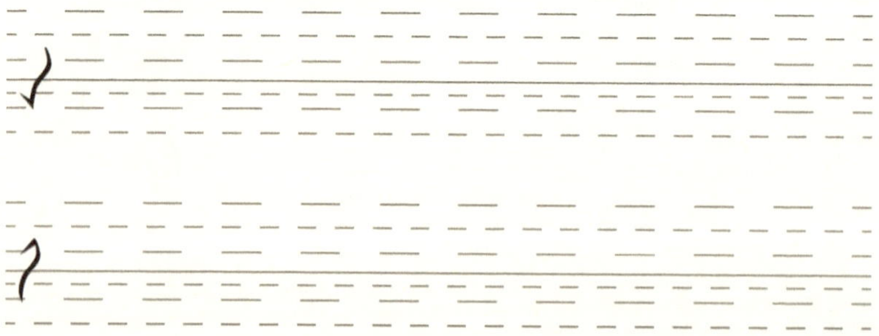

Useful words and phrases

hello	*y'znanĕthnofv*
please	*bvaal'*
thank you	*kh'dzarlo*
yes	*kthĕ'*
no	*zot*
not	*ēst*
How are you?	*mēfvamo ?shĕts?*
I am well.	*mofvēmo nĕth ay'mdĕ.*
I am not well.	*mofvēmo nĕth ēst ay'mdĕ.*
How does one say _____?	
	momo zarnth _____ ?shĕts?
What is that?	*yĕbvmo ?ĕbvu?*
I do not know.	*mofvēmo ja(h)rash ēst.*
I do not understand.	
	mofvēmo chooth ēst.

When do we eat?

hazurshtu ?ubvafv?

The meal was very good.

hazathramo fvē nĕthy'klo y'zl (h)ro.

Where is the WC?

soshyatafvēmo adzabvkthocha ?ashafv?

Turn left.

kth'saoch ushĕ go'nu fvē.

Turn right.

kth'saoch ushĕ gĕn' fvē.

Who is that?

yĕbvmo ?mobvu?

Who are they?

moomomo ?mobvu'm?

What is your name?

g(h)romfvĕ mēfvĕ ?ĕbvu?

My name is _____.

g(h)romfvĕ mēfvĕ nĕth _____.

May I introduce _____?

ushzarch _____ ?mofvēmo putch?

Have you seen my partner?

modza mĕfvĕ ?apchgo woshlo?

Is there coffee?

chē'tsa lĕ ?nĕth kthĕfvmo?

When will coffee be ready?

chē'tsamo lĕ nĕth psutakth' al'sto ?ubvafv?

May I have a coffee?

(h)rash chē'tsa aa ?mofvēmo putch?

May I have another coffee?

(h)rash chē'tsa chĕ aa ?mofvēmo putch?

Will you (pl.) have coffee or tea?

chē'tsa lĕ oo totsa lĕ ?(h)rashtu psutaktho?

Would you like to dance?

(h)ros'th ?momofvēmo putchtu?

I have not yet had coffee.

mofvēmo apch (h)rashlo ēst pĕ chē'tsa lĕ.

Let's go.　　*bvĕdzanth shosh momofvē.*

Goodbye　　*kth'nĕth ay'mdĕ*

Dzut!　　*!dzut!*

Verbs

Dvarsh features two verb conjugations, the *falling* and the *rising*. Conjugated forms carry information about a subject's person and number. Subject pronouns tend to be used only when clarity requires. It is not wrong to use them, but it is often unnecessary.

The falling conjugation includes verbs ending in

↷	*něth*
↶	*(h)rash*
↶	*ch'ch*
↶	*aath*

The rising conjugation includes verbs ending in

↷	*wosh*
↶	*shosh*

In written Dvarsh the verb root is pronounced the same in all conjugated forms. Stress may shift depending on where the root falls among the syllables, but values of the roots as characters do not shift as they do when a verb is adapted into a noun or adjective.

The Present - the Falling Conjugation

⌇   *nĕth*   **to be**

⌇	*nĕth*	I am
⌇∽ᴏ	*nĕthktho*	you (s.) are
⌇	*nĕth*	it is
⌇⌇	*nĕthtu*	we are
⌇∽ᴏ⌇	*nĕthkthotu*	you (pl.) are
⌇⌇⌇	*nĕthy'tu*	they are

present participle   ⌇⌇   *nĕthtĕ*   being

⌇⌇   *tunch*   **to hunger**

⌇⌇	*tunch*	I hunger
⌇⌇∽ᴏ	*tunchktho*	you (s.) hunger
⌇⌇	*tunch*	it hungers
⌇⌇⌇	*tunchtu*	we hunger
⌇⌇∽ᴏ⌇	*tunchkthotu*	you (pl.) hunger
⌇⌇⌇	*tunchy'tu*	they hunger

present participle   ⌇⌇   *tunchtĕ*   hungering

Write the Dvarsh verb form for each of the following:

1. you (pl.) hunger _____

2. it is _____

3. you (pl.) are _____

4. we hunger _____

5. hungering _____

6. I am _____

7. you (s.) hunger _____

8. you (s.) are _____

9. being _____

10. they hunger _____

11. it hungers _____

12. we are _____

13. I hunger _____

14. they are _____

Note: All the present forms differ except the first & third persons singular, which are commonly distinguished with subject pronouns. The pronoun meaning, "I/me" is *mofvē* [ᨀᨀ], and the pronoun meaning "it" is *mo* [ᨀ]. When the pronoun is the subject of a verb, the suffix, *-mo* [ᨀᨀ] is attached. Thus, "I am," translates as *mofvēmo nĕth* [ᨀᨀᨀᨀ ᨀ], and "it is" translates as *momo nĕth* [ᨀᨀᨀ ᨀ].

21

The Present - the Rising Conjugation

Note: The Rising conjugation present differs from the Falling in the second person singular and plural, and the third person plural.

꒐	*shosh*	**to go**	
꒐		*shosh*	I go
꒐ꔪꙅ		*shoshgo*	you (s.) go
꒐		*shosh*	it goes
꒐ꘀ		*shoshtu*	we go
꒐ꔪꙅꘀ		*shoshgotu*	you (pl.) go
꒐ꔪ꘎ꘀ		*shoshg'tu*	they go
present participle	꒐ꘀ	*shoshtĕ*	going

ꗑꙅꕔ	*jowsh*	**to perceive**	
ꗑꙅꕔ		*jowsh*	I perceive
ꗑꙅꕔꔪꙅ		*jowshgo*	you (s.) perceive
ꗑꙅꕔ		*jowsh*	it perceives
ꗑꙅꕔꘀ		*jowshtu*	we perceive
ꗑꙅꕔꔪꙅꘀ		*jowshgotu*	you (pl.) perceive
ꗑꙅꕔꔪ꘎ꘀ		*jowshg'tu*	they perceive
present participle	ꗑꙅꕔꘀ	*jowshtĕ*	perceiving

Write the Dvarsh verb form for each of the following:

1. it perceives _____

2. you (pl.) perceive _____

3. we go _____

4. going _____

5. I perceive _____

6. you (s.) go _____

7. you (s.) perceive _____

8. perceiving _____

9. they go _____

10. it goes _____

11. we perceive _____

12. I go _____

13. they perceive _____

14. you (pl.) go _____

The Preterit - the Falling Conjugation

Note: The preterit is used for past action that was completed, things done at particular times.

⟩ *něth* **to be**

⟩ᘓᘓᘓ	*něthklo*	I was
⟩ᘓᘓᘓᘓ	*něthktholo*	you (s.) were
⟩⟩ᘓᘓᘓ	*něthy'klo*	it was
⟩ᘓᘓᘓᘓ	*něthklotu*	we were
⟩ᘓᘓᘓᘓᘓ	*něthktholotu*	you (pl.) were
⟩⟩ᘓᘓᘓᘓ	*něthy'klotu*	they were

past participle   ⟩ᘓ   *něthlo*   been

⟩ᘓᘓ *notch* **to sleep**

⟩ᘓᘓᘓᘓᘓ	*notchklo*	I slept
⟩ᘓᘓᘓᘓᘓ	*notchktholo*	you (s.) slept
⟩ᘓᘓᘓᘓᘓ	*notchy'klo*	it slept
⟩ᘓᘓᘓᘓᘓ	*notchklotu*	we slept
⟩ᘓᘓᘓᘓᘓ	*notchktholotu*	you (pl.) slept
⟩ᘓᘓᘓᘓᘓ	*notchy'klotu*	they slept

past participle   ⟩ᘓᘓᘓ   *notchlo*   slept

24

Write the Dvarsh verb form for each of the following:

1. we slept _____

2. slept (past participle) _____

3. I was _____

4. you (s.) slept _____

5. you (s.) were _____

6. been _____

7. they slept _____

8. it slept _____

9. we were _____

10. I slept _____

11. they were _____

12. you (pl.) slept _____

13. it was _____

14. you (pl.) were _____

The Preterit - the Rising Conjugation

ᘯ   *shosh*   **to go**

ᘯᔕᒍᕽ	*shoshglo*	I went
ᘯᔕᕽᒍᕽ	*shoshgolo*	you (s.) went
ᘯᔕᒍᵗᕽ	*shoshgl'o*	it went
ᘯᔕᒍᕽᒡ	*shoshglotu*	we went
ᘯᔕᕽᒍᕽᒡ	*shoshgolotu*	you (pl.) went
ᘯᔕᒍᵗᕽᒡ	*shoshgl'otu*	they went

past participle   ᔕᒍᕽ   *shoshlo*   gone

ᘜᵗᒍ   *ja'wsh*   **to sketch**

ᘜᵗᒍᔕᒍᕽ	*ja'wshglo*	I sketched
ᘜᵗᒍᔕᕽᒍᕽ	*ja'wshgolo*	you (s.) sketched
ᘜᵗᒍᔕᒍᵗᕽ	*ja'wshgl'o*	it sketched
ᘜᵗᒍᔕᒍᕽᒡ	*ja'wshglotu*	we sketched
ᘜᵗᒍᔕᕽᒍᕽᒡ	*ja'wshgolotu*	you (pl.) sketched
ᘜᵗᒍᔕᒍᵗᕽᒡ	*ja'wshgl'otu*	they sketched

past participle   ᘜᵗᒍᒍᕽ   *ja'wshlo*   sketched

Write the Dvarsh verb form for each of the following:

1. you (s.) went _____

2. you (s.) sketched _____

3. sketched (past participle) _____

4. they went _____

5. it went _____

6. we sketched _____

7. I went _____

8. they sketched _____

9. you (pl.) went _____

10. it sketched _____

11. you (pl.) sketched _____

12. we went _____

13. gone _____

14. I sketched _____

The Imperfect - the Falling Conjugation

Note: The imperfect is used for past actions with no definite end.

ٮ	*nĕth*	**to be**	
ٮככ,		*nĕthkl'*	I was, was being, or used to be
ٮככﻭﻝ,		*nĕthkthol'*	you (s.) were, were being, or used to be
ٮٮ,ככﻝ,		*nĕthy'kl'*	it was, etc.
ٮככﻝ,ﻝ		*nĕthkl'tu*	we were, etc.
ٮככﻭﻝ,ﻝ		*nĕthkthol'tu*	you (pl.) were, etc.
ٮٮ,ככﻝ,ﻝ		*nĕthy'kl'tu*	they were, etc.

gerund   ٮﻝ,   *nĕthl'*   being

ٯ	*(h)rash*	**to have**	
ٯככ,		*(h)rashkl'*	I had, was having, or used to have
ٯככﻭﻝ,		*(h)rashkthol'*	you (s.) had, etc.
ٯٮ,ככ,		*(h)rashy'kl'*	it had, etc.
ٯככﻝ,ﻝ		*(h)rashkl'tu*	we had, etc.
ٯככﻭﻝ,ﻝ		*(h)rashkthol'tu*	you (pl.) had, etc.
ٯٮ,ככﻝ,ﻝ		*(h)rashy'kl'tu*	they had, etc.

gerund   ٯﻝ,   *(h)rashl'*   having

28

Write the Dvarsh verb form for each of the following:

1. we used to have _____

2. having (gerund) _____

3. I was being _____

4. you (s.) used to have _____

5. you (s.) were being _____

6. being (gerund) _____

7. they were having _____

8. it used to have _____

9. we were being _____

10. I used to have _____

11. they used to be _____

12. you (pl.) were having _____

13. it was being _____

14. you (pl.) used to be _____

The Imperfect - the Rising Conjugation

ꞔ   *shosh*   **to go**

ꞔꞔ,	*shoshgl'*	I went, was going, or used to go
ꞔꞔ,	*shoshgol'*	you (s.) went, etc.
ꞔꞔ,	*shoshgl'l'*	it went, etc.
ꞔꞔ,	*shoshgl'tu*	we went, etc.
ꞔꞔ,	*shoshgol'tu*	you (pl.) went, etc.
ꞔꞔ,	*shoshgl'l'tu*	they went, etc.
gerund ꞔ,	*shoshl'*	going

ꞔ   *yush*   **to fall**

ꞔꞔ,	*yushgl'*	I fell, was falling, or used to fall
ꞔꞔ,	*yushgol'*	you (s.) fell, etc.
ꞔꞔ,	*yushgl'l'*	it fell, etc.
ꞔꞔ,	*yushgl'tu*	we fell, etc.
ꞔꞔ,	*yushgol'tu*	you (pl.) fell, etc.
ꞔꞔ,	*yushgl'l'tu*	they fell, etc.
gerund ꞔ,	*yushl'*	falling

Write the Dvarsh verb form for each of the following:

1. you (s.) used to fall _____

2. falling (gerund) _____

3. they were going _____

4. it used to go _____

5. we were falling _____

6. I was going _____

7. they used to fall _____

8. you (pl.) used to go _____

9. it was falling _____

10. you (pl.) were falling _____

11. we used to go _____

12. going (gerund) _____

13. I used to fall _____

14. you (s.) were going _____

The Future - the Falling Conjugation

⌒   *něth*   **to be**

⌒ ⌒	*něth psuta*	I shall be
⌒ ⌒ᴝᴏ	*něth psutaktho*	you (s.) will be
⌒ ⌒ᴝᴏ'	*něth psutakth'*	it will be
⌒ᴊ ⌒	*něthtu psuta*	we shall be
⌒ᴊ ⌒ᴝᴏ	*něthtu psutaktho*	you (pl.) will be
⌒ᴊ ⌒ᴝᴏ'	*něthtu psutakth'*	they will be

ᶺ   *ch'ch*   **to want**

ᶺ ⌒	*ch'ch psuta*	I shall want
ᶺ ⌒ᴝᴏ	*ch'ch psutaktho*	you (s.) will want
ᶺ ⌒ᴝᴏ'	*ch'ch psutakth'*	it will want
ᶺᴊ ⌒	*ch'chtu psuta*	we shall want
ᶺᴊ ⌒ᴝᴏ	*ch'chtu psutaktho*	you (pl.) will want
ᶺᴊ ⌒ᴝᴏ'	*ch'chtu psutakth'*	they will want

Note: The verb, *ch'ch* [ᶺ] also means, "to seek."

Write the Dvarsh verb form for each of the following:

1. we shall want _____

2. I shall be _____

3. you (pl.) will want_____

4. you (s.) will be _____

5. they will want _____

6. it will want _____

7. we shall be _____

8. I shall want _____

9. they will be _____

10. you (s.) will want _____

11. it will be _____

12. you (pl.) will be _____

The Future - the Rising Conjugation

ʒ *shosh* **to go**

ʒ ⁀	*shosh psuta*	I shall go
ʒ ⁀⁀ᵒ	*shosh psutago*	you (s.) will go
ʒ ⁀⁀ʾ	*shosh psutag'*	it will go
ʒⱼ ⁀	*shoshtu psuta*	we shall go
ʒⱼ ⁀⁀ᵒ	*shoshtu psutago*	you (pl.) will go
ʒⱼ ⁀⁀ʾ	*shoshtu psutag'*	they will go

⁀•ʋ *nawsh* **to happen**

⁀•ʋ ⁀	*nawsh psuta*	I shall happen
⁀•ʋ ⁀⁀ᵒ	*nawsh psutago*	you (s.) will happen
⁀•ʋ ⁀⁀ʾ	*nawsh psutag'*	it will happen
⁀•ʋⱼ ⁀	*nawshtu psuta*	we shall happen
⁀•ʋⱼ ⁀⁀ᵒ	*nawshtu psutago*	you (pl.) will happen
⁀•ʋⱼ ⁀⁀ʾ	*nawshtu psutag'*	they will happen

Write the Dvarsh verb form for each of the following:

1. it will go _____

2. we shall happen _____

3. I shall go _____

4. they will happen _____

5. you (pl.) will go _____

6. it will happen _____

7. you (s.) will happen _____

8. we shall go _____

9. I shall happen _____

10. you (s.) will go _____

11. you (pl.) will happen _____

12. they will go _____

Some other falling verbs

෨	*onth*	to live
෨	*arsh*	to take
෨	*bvĕtath*	to give
෨	*soch*	to listen
෨	*swĕth*	to taste
෨	*skthursh*	to hear
෨	*ja(h)rash*	to know
෨	*tsoch*	to thirst
෨	*kthoch*	to rest

Some other rising verbs

෨	*yoldzawsh*	to smile
෨	*fvalosh*	to walk
෨	*fvash*	to run
෨	*mushĕsh*	to touch
෨	*bvĕsh*	to come
෨	*wosh*	to see

Other ways of expressing time

Two verbs introduced earlier may combine with certain forms of other verbs to construct different ways of locating actions or conditions in time. Conjugated forms of *nĕth* [૨], "to be," and *shosh* [૨], "to go," can combine with the past participle, present participle or infinitive of another verb to expand the range of expression.

For instance, present, preterit or future forms of *nĕth* can combine with the present participle of another verb to express action in progress during the referenced time.

In the present: I am smiling

ᒧᑎᒍᵒ ᒋ ᒕᓄᒎᒎ.ᒍᒍᒉ   *mofvēmo nĕth yoldzawshtĕ*

In the past: you (s.) were resting

ᒋᒎᵒᒍᵒ ᒎᵒᒒᒉ.   *nĕthktholo kthochtĕ*

In the future: they will be listening

ᒋᒍᵗ ᒋᒎᵖᵎ ᒒᵒᒒᒉ.   *nĕthtu psutakth' sochtĕ*

A combination of present forms of *shosh* with infinitives of other verbs provides a common means of indicating future action, even though no future form is used.

you (pl.) go to walk ("you are going to walk")

ᒒᒎᵒᒉᵗ ᒋ.ᒍᵒᒒ   *shoshgotu fvalosh*

they go to listen ("they are going to listen")

ᒒᒎᵖᒉᵗ ᒒᵒᒒ   *shoshg'tu soch*

I go to see ("I am going to see")

ᒧᑎᒍᵒ ᒒ ᒍ   *mofvēmo shosh wosh*

Note: Both conjugations form the present participle by attaching the suffix -*tĕ* [ᒍᒉ] to a verb's infinitive.

The auxiliary verb *apch* [⸲ﮩﮩ]

Rising conjugation

	Singular		Plural	

present [has, have]

		Singular		Plural
1st	ﮩﮩ	*apch*	ﮩﮩ	*apchtu*
2nd	ﮩﮩ	*apchgo*	ﮩﮩ	*apchgotu*
3rd	ﮩﮩ	*apch*	ﮩﮩ	*apchtu*

preterit [had]

		Singular		Plural
1st	ﮩﮩ	*apchlo*	ﮩﮩ	*apchlotu*
2nd	ﮩﮩ	*apchlogo*	ﮩﮩ	*apchlogotu*
3rd	ﮩﮩ	*apchl'o*	ﮩﮩ	*apchl'otu*

future [shall have, will have]

		Singular		Plural
1st	ﮩﮩ	*apchp'*	ﮩﮩ	*apchp'tu*
2nd	ﮩﮩ	*apchp'go*	ﮩﮩ	*apchp'gotu*
3rd	ﮩﮩ	*apchp'ĕ*	ﮩﮩ	*apchp'ĕtu*

conditional [would have]

		Singular		Plural
1st	ﮩﮩ	*ēapchp'*	ﮩﮩ	*ēapchp'tu*
2nd	ﮩﮩ	*ēapchp'go*	ﮩﮩ	*ēapchp'gotu*
3rd	ﮩﮩ	*ēapchp'ĕ*	ﮩﮩ	*ēapchp'ĕtu*

Another verb useful for expanding the range of ways to locate action or condition in time is the auxiliary, *apch* [⸲ﮩﮩ]. It is an auxiliary because it is only used in combination with another verb. *Apch* is translated as "to have," but this is not "to have" in the sense of "to possess" or "to consume." The verb meaning "to have" in these senses is *(h)rash* [ﮩ]. The two are not equivalent.

Falling conjugation

	Singular	Plural
present [has, have]		
1st	apch	apchtu
2nd	apchktho	apchkthotu
3rd	apch	apchtu
preterit [had]		
1st	apchlo	apchlotu
2nd	apchloktho	apchloktu
3rd	apchl'o	apchl'otu
future [shall have, will have]		
1st	apchp'	apchp'tu
2nd	apchp'ktho	apchp'ktu
3rd	apchp'ĕ	apchp'ĕtu
conditional [would have]		
1st	ēapchp'	ēapchp'tu
2nd	ēapchp'ktho	ēapchp'ktu
3rd	ēapchp'ĕ	ēapchp'ĕtu

In practice, conjugated forms of *apch* combine with the past participle or infinitive of another verb. There are differences in how *apch* is conjugated depending upon the conjugation of the other verb. On these pages *apch* is shown in four commonly used tenses in rising and falling forms.

Note: the past participle is formed by attaching the suffix -*lo* [ℐ℮] to a verb's infinitive.

Examples of *apch* in combination:

I have to rest
mofvēmo apch kthoch

We had listened
apchlotu sochlo

You (sing.) will have heard
apchp'ktho skthurshlo

It had happened
apchl'o nawshlo

You (pl.) will have to run
apchp'ktu fvash

They would have walked
ēapchp'ĕtu fvaloshlo

Write the Dvarsh for each of the following:

1. it had touched _____

2. they were wanting _____

3. I have to know _____

4. you (s.) will have seen _____

5. we are going to smile _____

6. it will be touching _____

7. you (pl.) are going to fall _____

8. you (s.) had to be _____

9. they will have gone _____

40

10. they would have to walk _____

11. I am going to listen _____

12. we have to smile _____

13. you (s.) are going to be _____

14. it had to happen _____

15. we have to be _____

16. we would have to smile _____

17. it will have touched _____

18. you (s.) had seen _____

19. it was sleeping _____

20. we were being _____

21. they are hearing _____

22. you (s.) have to be _____

23. they have known _____

24. it is going to happen _____

25. they have to walk _____

26. I will be listening _____

27. it has to happen _____

28. you (s.) were seeing _____

29. we would have been _____

30. I have listened _____

31. they had wanted _____

32. you (pl.) had to fall _____

33. it had to sleep _____

34. you (pl.) have to run _____

35. they are going to know _____

36. you (pl.) will have heard _____

37. I will have to listen _____

38. I had run _____

Pronouns

Because of the way in which Dvarsh verbs conjugate, subject pronouns are unnecessary in many situations. A notable exception is in the present tense, where first and third persons singular are identical. It is not wrong to use subject pronouns in other situations, but it is wordy.

Dvarsh uses the same pronouns for subject and object, but when used as a subject the suffix -*mo* [᠊ᠥ] attaches to the pronoun, the same as with a noun.

Personal pronouns include:

I/me	*mofvē*	᠗ᠥ	we/us	*momofvē*	᠗᠗ᠥ
you	*mēfva*	᠗:ᠺ.	you	*mēfva'm*	᠗:ᠺ.'ᠥ
it	*mo*	᠗	they/them	*moomo*	᠗ᠲᠥ᠗

Demonstrative pronouns include:

this	*bvum*	ᠥᠲ᠗	these	*bvum'm*	ᠥᠲ᠗'ᠥ
that	*yĕbv*	ᠺ:ᠥ	those	*yĕbv'm*	ᠺ:ᠥ'ᠥ

Relative pronouns include:

that	*yĕbv*	ᠺ:ᠥ	what	*ĕbvu*	:ᠥᠲ
which	*dvabvu*	᠌ᠥᠲ	which	*dvabvu'm*	᠌ᠥᠲ'ᠥ
who/whom (s.)	*mobvu*	ᠥᠥᠲ	(pl.)	*mobvu'm*	ᠥᠥᠲ'ᠥ

Note: the third person singular pronoun, *mo* [᠗], is gender neutral, and may be translated as either "it" or "that individual." On those occasions when clarity demands gender distinction (less often than one may imagine), the pronoun is modified by the adjectives, *ag* [.ᠥ] "female," *u'g* [ᠲ.ᠥ] "male," or *ēgo* [:ᠥᠥ] "neuter."

Write the Dvarsh for each of the following:

1. You (s.) heard me _____

2. I see them _____

3. They will have seen it _____

4. It touched us _____

5. We saw you (pl.) _____

6. You (pl.) have to hear her _____

7. She knows this _____

8. This gives that _____

9. That is him _____

10. He goes to see you (s.) _____

11. You (s.) taste those _____

12. Those would have perceived us _____

13. We will hear whom? _____

14. Who sees you (pl.)? _____

15. You (pl.) have to have these _____

16. These want me _____

Word lists

Adjective pairs:

back	aglaa	⌁⌁..	front	az'gla	.⌁,⌁⌁.
bad	alēshl'	.⌁:⌁⌁,	good	y'zl	⌁⌁
big	spĕk	⌁⌁:.⌁	little	spakzl	⌁⌁.⌁⌁⌁
cold	atsētht'	.⌁:⌁⌁,	hot	hĕts	⌁:.⌁
down	sobv	⌁⌁⌁	up	sĕk	⌁:.⌁
each	fvamt	⌁.⌁⌁	every	bvamt	⌁.⌁⌁
far	apsy'	.⌁⌁'	near	ushl'	,⌁⌁,
female	ag	.⌁	male	u'g	,⌁⌁
few	ēmomumu	:⌁⌁⌁,⌁,	many	m'momumu	⌁,⌁⌁,⌁,
high	arsĕk	.⌁⌁:.⌁	low	aso'bv	.⌁⌁,⌁
thick	spochtĕ	⌁⌁⌁⌁:.	thin	th'l	⌁,⌁
inner	ma(h)r'	⌁.⌁'	outer	aēy'	.:⌁'
left	o'gnu	⌁,⌁⌁,	right	agn'	.⌁⌁,

Other adjectives

a, an	aa	..
able	ajushl'	.⌁,⌁⌁,
dark	azēna	.⌁:⌁.
later	apsl'	.⌁⌁,
light	gozul	⌁⌁⌁,⌁
middle	asmonta	.⌁⌁⌁⌁⌁.
no	zot	⌁⌁⌁
private	alēhota	.⌁:⌁⌁.
public	azuta	.⌁,⌁.

45

some	*lĕ*	◡..
some	*alĕm*	.◡..◠
the	*fvē*	◠ (also ◠:)
warm	*ĕchĕts*	..◈.◡
well	*ay'mdĕ*	◠'◠◡..

Note: *Lĕ* [◡..] is generally used for an indeterminate specific (i.e. "one day") or a portion of something not countable (i.e. "coffee," as opposed to "a coffee"). *Alĕm* [.◡..◠] is generally used for unspecified quantities of countable things (i.e. "some people").

Note: Adjectives always agree in number with the noun modified.

A smatter of adverbs:

about	*n'lu*	◠◡ₑ
again	*ĕbvĕ*	..◔..
always	*bvafvom*	◔.◠◠
ever	*ubvmĕ*	◠◔..
far	*pay'*	◠.◠'
how	*shĕts*	◔..◡
later	*apsl'*	.◠◡'
less	*ēchĕ*	:◈..
more	*chĕ*	◈..
near/nearly	*ushl'*	ₑ◡◡'
never	*ēbvafv*	:◔.◠
no	*zot*	◡ₒ◡
now	*bvanh*	◔.◠
not	*ēst*	:◈◡
over	*losĕ*	◡ₒ◈..
ready	*al'sto*	.◡◈◡ₒ

46

so	*chul*	
still	*psĕ*	
that	*yĕbv*	
then	*bvafvu*	
there	*kthĕfv*	
under	*lēchl'*	
very	*(h)ro*	
well	*y'mdz'*	
what	*ĕbvu*	
when	*ubvafv*	
where	*ashafv*	
why	*shok*	
yes	*kthĕ'*	
yet	*pĕ*	

Colors (adjective form, left; noun form, right)

black	*azēnlo*	*zēnlo*
blue	*akthabvl'*	*kthabv*
blue-green	*akthatw'*	*kthatw'*
brown	*atwĕzlo*	*twĕzlo*
green	*atow'*	*tow'*
orange	*ahĕznal*	*hĕznal*
pink	*hĕzuul*	*hĕzuuldĕ*
purple	*aho'kth'*	*ho'kth'*
red	*ahĕzlo*	*hĕzlo*
white	*awomuzl*	*womozl*
yellow	*ahodv*	*hodv*

Conjunctions:

and / plus	*ota*	℧
because	*něbvo*	
but	*ēta*	
if	*nup'*	
or	*oo*	
so	*'t*	
yet	*'pě*	

Courtesies:

Dzut!	*dzut!*	
goodbye	*kth'něth ay'mdě*	
hello	*y'znaněthnofv*	
how are you?	*měfvamo ?shěts?*	
I am well.	*mofvēmo něth ay'mdě.*	
May I?	*?mofvēmo putch?*	
please	*bvaal'*	
thank you	*kh'dzarlo*	

Possession

its	*měě*	
my / mine	*měfvě*	
our / ours	*moměfvě*	
their / theirs	*m'omě*	
whose	*mobvufvě*	
yours (s.)	*měfvě*	
yours (pl.)	*m'měfvě*	

Prepositions:

as/like	*ě'*	∴'
at/with	*o'*	၄'
by	*lo'*	၁၄'
for	*ch'*	⋌'
from/of	*oa*	၄.
in/on	*'a*	'.
through	*(h)ru*	၁၅
to	*ushě*	၎ၡ∴

Simple times:

autumn	*mwafvě*	၁၂⌒∴
dawn	*hězot*	၁∴၂၄၁
day	*tazl*	၁ၡ
dusk	*tazlět*	၁ၡ၁∴၁
midnight	*asmontatalo*	.⋌၁၄⌒၁၁၁၄
moment	*lě(h)r't'*	၁∴၁'၁
morning	*ēpmonta*	∶⌒⌒၄⌒၁.
night	*talo*	၁၁၄
noon	*asmontatazl*	.⋌၁၄⌒၁၁၁ၡ
spring	*tutfvě*	၁ၟ၁⌒∴
summer	*yědfvě*	⌒∴⋋⌒∴
today	*tazum*	၁ၡ၌⌒
tomorrow	*tashopa*	၁ၟ၄⌒.
winter	*tsětfvě*	၁∶၁⌒∴
year	*lothgo*	၁၄⅔⌒၄
yesterday	*tazěps*	၁ၡ∶⌒

49

Nouns for the traveler

bakery	*yadthĕtha*	
bar/pub	*habyĕts ērmol*	
bed	*hatcha*	
beer	*spapĕrmlot*	
bicycle	*bvasĕthot*	
blanket	*m'sha*	
bowl	*shakyo*	
bread	*hatzl*	
building	*thl'*	
chair/seat	*tsultok*	
child	*gopo*	
coffee	*chē'tsa*	
coffee shop	*fvĕghachē'tsa*	
crow	*mosmokbvĕcha*	
crows	*mosmokbvēch'm*	
cup	*tsabvya*	
door	*hogyo*	
field	*hazucha*	
food	*hazl*	
forest	*gagops*	
fork	*hazya*	
friend	*hutha*	
friends	*huth'm*	
fruit	*yups*	
hill	*chĕg*	

hills	*chĕg'm*	
house	*habyĕts*	
ice	*tsēt*	
inn	*yata*	
journey	*soshosha*	
knife	*hazw'ot*	
lake	*ts'not*	
lover	*dzwoshót*	
mate/partner	*modza*	
meal	*hazathra*	
music	*sokthadz*	
name	*g(h)romfvĕ*	
orangutan	*mos'hojēnl'*	
parent	*th'ngúk*	
path	*sos*	
plate	*h'yaga*	
pot	*yadvom*	
rain	*kyusha*	
road	*sa*	
room	*hachona*	
sky	*ktho*	
spoon	*yoya*	
table	*thoga*	
taco	*takho*	
tea	*totsa*	
tea shop	*fvĕghatotsa*	

51

train	*moshom*	ᓂᕐᕉᕥ
transportation	*yoy'měsha*	ᓂᓂᕐᕘᕬᕁ
water	*ts'na*	ᕕ
WC	*soshyatafvēmo adzabvkthocha*	
	ᕥᕠᕬᕑᕟᕬᕥ ᕑᕎᕟᕥᕁ	
window	*kthashtyo*	ᕥᕗᕰᕥ
worker	*sělutha*	ᕣᕐᕥ
wine	*yupěmlot*	ᓂᕈᕬᕂᕥᕍᕑ

Verb sampler

to be	*něth*	ᕁ
to be able	*ajush*	ᕎᕗ
to begin	*gabvath*	ᕣᕟᕣ
to build / to make	*aath*	ᕣ
to choose	*fvēth*	ᕂᕣ
to come	*bvěsh*	ᕟᕁᕗ
to dance	*(h)ros'th*	ᕥᕣᕟ
to eat	*hazursh*	ᕥᕎᕑ
to fall	*yush*	ᕁᕗ
to find	*jaz'th*	ᕎᕎᕣ
to give	*bvětath*	ᕟᕰᕖᕣ
to go	*shosh*	ᕗ
to happen	*nawsh*	ᕁᕎ
to have	*(h)rash*	ᕥ
to have (aux. v.)	*apch*	ᕁᕣ
to hear	*skthursh*	ᕣᕥᕑ
to hunger	*tunch*	ᕖᕁᕣ

to introduce	ushzarch	ˌꙅꙅꙅꙅ
to know	ja(h)rash	ꙅꙅ
to lead	gěj'nth	ꙅꙅꙅ
to like	dzututh	ꙅꙅꙅ
to listen	soch	ꙅꙅꙅ
to live	onth	ꙅꙅ
to love	dzwosh	ꙅꙅꙅꙅ
to make/to build	aath	ꙅ
may (aux. v.)	putch	ꙅꙅꙅ
to meet	omth	ꙅꙅꙅ
to perceive	jowsh	ꙅꙅꙅ
to put	lěhath	ꙅꙅꙅꙅ
to rest	kthoch	ꙅꙅꙅ
to rise	kthěsh	ꙅꙅꙅ
to run	fvash	ꙅꙅ
to say	zarnth	ꙅꙅꙅ
to see	wosh	ꙅ
to seek/to want	ch'ch	ꙅ
to sketch	ja'wsh	ꙅꙅ
to sleep	notch	ꙅꙅꙅ
to smile	yoldzawsh	ꙅꙅꙅꙅ
to stop	ēsh	ꙅꙅ
to take	arsh	ꙅꙅ
to talk	ojlēnth	ꙅꙅꙅꙅ
to taste	swěth	ꙅꙅꙅ
to thirst	tsoch	ꙅꙅꙅ

to touch	*mushĕsh*	
to turn	*saoch*	
to wait	*ēlo'sh*	
to walk	*fvalosh*	
to want/to seek	*ch'ch*	

Sentences

Write the Dvarsh for each of the following:
[literal translation of Dvarsh idioms is in brackets, where needed]

1. We came by train yesterday.

_____

2. I took a room at the inn.

_____

3. Will you (s.) have coffee or tea? [Coffee or tea ?will you have?]

_____

4. How are you (pl.) today [Today ?you are how?]

_____

5. Orangutans like fruit, but do not like coffee.

_____

6. How is her/his parent? [Her/his parent ?how?]

_____

7. Her/his parent is not well.

_____

8. Their child has taken the path through the forest.

_____

9. It (the child) is walking to the lake.

_____

10. Would you (s.) like to live here? [To live here ?you would like?]

_____

11. May I have two tacos and coffee? [Two tacos and coffee ?I may have?]

_____

12. You (pl.) will have to run to the tea shop from here.

_____

13. The orangutan has a red bicycle.

_____

14. At the bar, you may have beer but she/he will have tea.

_____

15. I am hungry. When will the meal be ready? [I hunger. The meal will be ready ?When?]

_____

16. There is a pink and yellow blanket on the bed.

_____

17. The table near the window has three chairs.

_____

18. This morning we went to the coffee shop.

_____

19. Tonight we shall dance in the bar near the tall hill.

_____

20. The sky is blue now, but tomorrow may have rain.

_____

21. She has a plate and a fork. I have a bowl and a spoon.

_____

22. The bakery is the purple building near the coffee shop.

_____

23. That is purple. It is not blue-green.

_____

24. Yesterday was warm. Today is hot. Tomorrow may be cold.

_____

25. My friend fell on the path and wants to rest.

_____

26. We like the lake but the water is cold.

_____

27. They had dark beer with the orangutan at the bar.

_____

28. At midnight you wanted wine.

_____

29. When you were a child you sought a crow for a friend.

_____

Reading and Translation

58

STIKMANTICA

Words, Images & Other Artifacts

A Hidden World Reaches Out.

Stikmantica online

- ﹖ language resources
- ﹖ cultural notes
- ﹖ "Musings" blog
- ﹖ design scrapbooks
- ﹖ announcements
- ﹖ music & other audio
- ﹖ video links
- ﹖ newsletter signup
- ﹖ catalog of titles
- ﹖ oddments

ROBERTSTIKMANZ.COM • STIKMANTICA.COM • DVARSH.ORG

www.ingramcontent.com/pod-product-compliance
Lightning Source LLC
Chambersburg PA
CBHW030655110726
47901CB00002B/722